Over 100 POEMS
ON Faith and Victory

James Safo

LLM(Master of Laws o/g), BA (Hons),Cert Ed,

Psy.N, GN, Dip Crim, Cert Acct. Dip H& S

All Rights Reserved

Disclaimer (Exclusive Clause)

The author and all employees disclaim any incorrect interpretation wrong answers to questions or text, harm including emotional, psychological and physical or any form of harm to the reader/listener or being given information by third parties. Furthermore, this disclaimer protects all contributory people, directors, employees, 3rd parties and the author and will not be liable for any injury caused.

Dedication

I dedicate this book to my granddaughters

Kristelle, Lilley, Alice and Ruby and

grandson Donnell

Preface

Over 100 poems are inspiration on Faith and Victory, which cover most arears, from Believing in Almighty God, facing challenges or difficulties and eventually victory is achieved. Faith can be related to "3P" patience, persistence and perseverance which in most cases result victory. Faith can be destroyed by fear or doubt, example, Peter had a little faith and was able to walk on the sea, but as soon as he doubted he lost his faith and he began to sink, luckily he was saved by Jesus. All the poems are written in modern English language, and in some of them I have broken the rules to express what I wish to say and to allow my readers to understand the inner feeling. All religious faiths books emphasise on having faith in the supreme Almighty God is paramount. In fact the Bible verse states figuratively, that if you have faith then you can move mountain to the sea. By faith all the messengers of God survived ordeal and became victorious. There are 4 poems books that I have written and published; 1) "The ONE" 130 variety poems, 2) over 200 Love poems and over 100 love ice breakers 3) over 100 Poems on racism, discrimination and suffering 4) over 100 poems on faith and victory. My formula to heaven is; Forgive and Love everyone, then Believe, trust and have faith in God is the key to heaven

About the Author

Although I was brought up as a Roman Catholic, I believe in all major religion who worship only God or Allah or whatever name one might use for the Almighty God. All my undertaken in life had been by Faith. From as an abandon child to one of most successful in Europe. Lost all my wealth but with faith, I regain more than twice what I had, in fact in some cases by faith I got more than 10 times.

My qualifications include master's degree in Laws, BA(Hons) in law and accounts, lecturer Cert Ed, qualified general and psychiatry nurse, counselling and a lot more as listed at the end of this publication.

Have solely written and published over 30 titles books on all major religious faiths in the world, books on academic; Law, accounts, criminology, counselling, business (4 books), psychology, health, Poems (4 books) etc.

Some of the religion books been translated from English into Arabic, chines, French and Spanish.

Chapter 1

Chapter 2

FAITH POEMS

1

WHAT IS FAITH?

(James Safo)

Many call it a believe,
Other refers to it as tolerance.
But what is faith,
what becomes of life without it?

Faith justifies a person,
By it everyone lives,
Faith sanctifies our everyday life,
By faith, we find a reason to live,
To hold on when the going gets tough.

Faith is the hope for unknown,
it gives us assurance and fulfilment,
As the saying goes,
Faith without action is dead,
Faith does not eliminate the urge for hard work,
Live by faith, walk by faith but,
do the much you can.

HOPELESSNESS.

(James Safo)

At times, my hopes dwindle,

All my dreams seem shuttered,

I find no answer,

The question why me,

Dominate my mind,

But I still hang onto my faith.

God is just I believe,

He makes no mistakes,

When storms come our way,

And trials of whatever form,

In faith, we find solace,

That no storm lasts forever.

When no solution seems to work,

In Gods' grace do I rest,

When friends abandon me,

And all in life seems meaningless,

In my Almighty Father, I find comfort.

He is everlasting,

Beyond all human understanding,

He sees all our struggles,

And all our dark corners.
He makes no mistakes,
Have faith and trust in him.

FROM PEACE TO PIECES.
(James Safo)

Once I lived happily,

But now am broken by the trials of life,

I am badly beaten,

My joy and peace blown to by the winds,

To you Almighty father,

I surrender my broken pieces.

You will make them,

Back to my usual peace,

You are full of sweet grace,

No one comes to you and,

Leaves empty handed.

My life seems hopeless,

Struggle and pain are the new norm,

You are Alpha and Omega,

Everlasting you can fix my pieces,

You can restore them once more,

Make my life peaceful restored living.

4

DADDY'S TEARS.

(James Safo)

Today you are breaking the cultural norm day,

A dad does not cry before the children,

But what am seeing makes me cry more,

I am not mocking you daddy,

It is very hard,

Yes times are and hand you have been through

Hell.

Today for the first time in my thirty years,

I am seeing you dad sob in great pain,

I don't mean to hurt or make a joking of the,

Situation,

But dad you seem like a three years old,

Your height of six feet is an illusion before this

Situation.

Dad you have lost a thing of great treasure,

It means life to you,

I can see it right into your eyes,

You are not the usual brave and courageous man

I have known,

It makes me to want to cry too,

The pain of losing someone you have loved for,

Decades,

For sure love knows no age,

The woman you have loved and introduced to me

As my stepmother,

How you held your arms around her in cool love,

She has at last betrayed you for another,

Shoulder.

Being a big papa's gal,

I know how it feels when love is betrayed,

You used to hug her for you cherished her,

But dad I want to know that all is not lost,

As girl you have adopted from the streets,

My love for you is unconditional,

Oh dad be calm and smile.

MY TEARS

(James Safo)

My life-long dream is lost
No one is trying to find me
Not even my beloved friends and relatives.
My story has turned upside down
All what fills my mind is "I wish I knew"

My teacher and parents played their part,
Daily parental guidance and teacher's counsel
To you may friends I lay my blame
For you introduced me to it
You called it *weed*
Little did I know it would shun my dreams.

That time behind the dormitories and in the
washrooms
We had the best of moments as a team
One puff made it feel like heaven
Little would I know that it will turnout as hell.
Without wanting to be left behind,
I became a crucial member of the crew.

My dream was to become a doctor
But where am I today?

Rehabilitation centre my so longed for university,
All my life gone with the dogs.

Oh my little brothers if you care to listen.
Am wishing that you could make it better.
Rubbish the kind of friends
Who would lead to harm substance use.
Please if you care live your life
and accomplish your dreams.

LAUGH AND THE WORLD LAUGHS BACK

(James Safo)

Does the old caring world exist?

Back then they said

Laugh and the world will laugh with you

Weed and the whole world will cry with you.

Gone are the days

The world and people have changed.

Today you sing and the hills remain silent.

Gone are the days when the hills sung back.

What a messy and noisy world were living.

No one seems to care about the other.

Them are the days.

When you smiled and the world smiled back

When you grieved and the earth grieved with

you.

Everyone is busy

Busy with their lousy selfish life.

Everyone seeking their measure of pleasure.

They are less concerned with your censored life.

Here comes the bare truth

That no one lie with you when you die.

7

THE INFINITE GRACE
(James Safo)

Great is the Grace of God,

To suffer fallen humanity,

Time and again a chance,

Demonstrating his unending love.

Great is the Grace of the Almighty,

Searching the lost, forgiving iniquities,

Empowering wretched souls,

Bring all into harmony with the Maker.

Great is the Grace of the Creator,

Manifesting his love for mankind,

To share in his glory everlasting,

Restoring the kingdom everlasting to humanity.

Great is the Grace of the Great King,

Exceeding all sin and all guilt,

You that desire to see His Face,

Hearken to the call, receive His infinite Grace.

THE ONLY RELIGION

(James Safo)

Often it's told,
Of the religions of the world,
A race in numbers and dominion and flair,
The true religion is love.

Often it's told,
Of the Great and Greatest prophets,
A race for large followings, and pomp,
Devoid of love, tells of the emptiness.

Often it's told,
Of defending religion to death,
By death, gun, bomb knife,
The Seed of hatred is enmity to Creator.

Of love for one another,
No race, language culture, origin,
Of the dignity of all humanity,
Of the unconditional love for humanity, is the only
religion.

9

THE AXE IS READY
(James Safo)

Oh man of God, upon the Gates,

Sound the Trumpet, war is coming,

The City is no longer safe,

The time of visitation is nigh.

The Soldiers of the Almighty cometh,

The axe is ready, the Master has commanded,

Every tree, fruits of repentance to bear,

Or be cut down at visitation.

The day of Great Ululation,

Of fear and Grieve and fear for mockers,

A day of celebration for King's children,

For the Redemption has been longed.

Oh man of the Almighty,

Duty dispensed, warnings given,

The City of sin will be overrun,

The axe is fitted not in vain; the command is sure.

THE KINGDOM COME
(James Safo)

The Glory of our King,
The Holy Books tell,
Our eyes shall behold,
Forever we shall rejoice.

The Kingdom of our Lord,
Of Peace, Love, harmony,
No pain, death or separation
Forever we shall be restored.

The Kingdom of our Lord,
Uncertainties shall be no more,
Is nigh at hand, is come for all,
Forever we shall be restored.

The Kingdom of our King,
A call to join in the glory,
Is extended, the mercy is come,
Forever we shall rejoice with the King.

11

OUR ONLY HOPE
(James Safo)

They pride in the modernized weaponry,

We are rat timid in their eyes,

They pride in armies and chariots,

We pride in our Lord.

We indeed are minced meat,

Before their machineries and art,

The art of war, widely studied,

Our Lord lifts us in our weakness.

Our eyes may not see,

For we are awed by pompous armies,

But mighty and countless are His armies,

Unseen, protecting His beloved forever.

They pride in their chariots,

They threaten with their armies,

Enemies shall design wart schemes,

He shall scatter them, our only Hope.

BRING THEM TO THE FOLD.

(James Safo)

The war rages on, darkness and light,

Bring them in, to share in bright,

Glory of Kingdom come, Master's command,

Choose to adhere, bring them to the fold.

The harvest is ripe, tarry no more,

Go to cities, mountains, villages evermore,

Tell them the time, the invitation live,

Choose to adhere, bring them to the fold.

Armed with the word, rather than guns and bombs,

Deeply grounded, learned in doctrine,

Showing mercy kindness, just as received,

Choose to adhere, bring them to the fold.

13

THE CERTAINTY OF HOPE.

(James Safo)

The promise given, thousands years ago,

A Kingdom of Glory, the chosen to go,

To rest, cure, joy, reign with Glorious King,

Time gone long, diminishing hope in thing.

Many soldiers of faith, clinging to hope passed,

Others came and fought, too no more passed,

Generations after generations, strength diminishing,

Of clinging on, abandoning oath of race keeping.

Stricken by calamities, life unbearable indeed,

Wondering of the promises, validity and deed,

Lost in worries and fears, currently loss of faith,

Of clinging on, abandoning oath of race keeping.

The last resort, the Lords assurance of character,

Never changing in words, promises, deeds character,

What He says he accomplishes, certainty of word

Bold assurance to cling on, for the Hope is certain.

OUR ROCK, OUR REFUGE.

(James Safo)

The mighty rock, the refuge of all,
The seasoned fighter, battle never lost,
Calling upon all, trust to found,
On the Mighty Rock, fortress.

Redeeming His faithful, historical wars,
Records chronicled, encourage in woes,
Words of truth testifying, Powers to Redeem,
Those who trust, surrender fit deem.

The one who guides, has guided nations,
Ancient chosen people, wrought mightily,
Seeks to encompass, protection to His,
Those who trust, surrender fit deem.

The Song of praise, encouragement all nations,
Great, might, wealth, hopeless dependent donations,
The Might one of war, Our rock, refuge,
Withstands all resistance, delivers sure victory.

15

LAMENTATIONS COMING.

(James Safo)

The cried from the North, the Day of visitation nigh,

Sitting on throne, armed with sword high,

King's visitation time, correct the err,

Judgment upon earth come, destruction to sinners,

Mockers and despisers, trembling in belly,

Trembling like pebbles, teething biting chilly,

The islands moved, mountains trembling fear,

The Great king of North comes who to Stand.

Like lightning, the Glory seen everywhere,

Escorted by Angels host, Chariots of fire everywhere,

Armed to teeth, war raging on sinners,

The Great Day, Judgment of earth cometh.

Fleeing multitudes, to mountains and caves,

Fearing glory, hiding from his face,

Once bold and opposes, now cowardly weak,

The fate of ignorant, warnings given unheeded.

JEWELS FOR MASTER

(James Safo)

The treasures of inspiration, chronicled to save seed,
Warnings and admonitions, checking next' deed,
Saving the world, consequences of rotten society.
Society of diversity, standards lowered daily.

Train up child, duty placed in parents,
Society as well partakes, secure like patents,
They ways of Heaven, instruct at tender age,
When years catch up, divine path to keep.

Sing in the morning evening, remind them of Lord,
To appreciate live health, isn't common occurrence,
Molded by Almighty, upheld kept in fold,
Crediting science not, same benefits from Ordinance.

The fruits to see, in life even eternity,
Of instructions given, command heeded,
Dutifully executed, character molded.
Jewels for Master presented eternal reward.

17

MOVE FORWARD

(James Safo)

You just have to keep that spirit,

And wait for the right time to come,

Things will be better with time,

Things will get on with light

Face the world with being bright,

Then go and have up that might.

What do you fear today?

Of things that happened yesterday,

Take each day with that smile,

Stay happy all the way and while,

That will surely change your life,

Do worry about things matter in life,

There is sunlight on your window,

Then why do you always see the dark,

There is so much to see around,

Why can't you see that spark?

Life will be tough for you,

Life will also give you a clue.

18

PERSEVERANCE

(James Safo)

Think about things that make a difference,

For life is as wonderful as you see,

 Smile because you have a reason,

To be happy you don't need a season,

There might be days when you may want to shout,

But you are certainly not out.

And if you keep patience in that hour,

You can surely reach for that brightest star,

So, keep patience and that will give you peace of mind,

It will make you a better person and kind,

Sorrows and happiness go along the way,

You can't have a middle way.

Face your sorrows with acceptance and smile,

Because they are going to stay for a while,

Hold on to happiness coz that matters a lot,

It will remain in the most pedant thought,

It's a feeling that goes all along the life,

Whenever you find reasons, or you strive.

You never realize the difference in right and wrong,

When you believe that you are strong,

Situations can sometimes go against the tide,

And you look for a place to hide,

Face the world with being bright,

Then go and have up that might,

Things will go along in your way,

And you will also have your say.

19

POSITIVE TOGETHER.

(James Safo)

We bond over a cup of tea, and gel over charades,
In every healthy argument, our knowledge only
upgrades,
We share our sorry times, and all the days of glee,
We all are bonded by love and smiles, all for free.

When the roots shake, the branches lend a hand,
One helps the other and other helps another,
Every soft heart and clear voice, to help understand,
People who teaches and learns together.

What if the things are wrong?
You know that you are strong,
What if the light is dim?
And the situation is grim.

You think positive and everything will be fine,
That is the only prayer in life, it is really divine,
When you will feel so good,
So, keep smiling all the way.

You need to find yourself and explore,
You need to settle all the woes,

Don't look back as yesterday is gone,

Look at the bright future that will come.

20

LIFE IS UP AND DOWN.

(James Safo)

Your way can also be the same,

But if you only blame,

So, don't turn behind and see,

Life is waiting for you to thee.

Trust yourself and stay as you are,

There are times to change and far.

But, if you are cool things will also leave you,

You will have your way in too,

Sometimes you may feel down and out,

Sometimes you may feel left out of the crowd,

That does not mean that you have to feel sad,

Things can be really bad

 Happiness is a state to which you belong,

But it's your calling to be strong,

Happiness begins with a positive mind,

It leaves you in things you can't find.

Life will give you something to cheer my dear,

Stay positive and you will be able to let go of all your

fear,

Be positive and you will find a reason,

Of staying happy in each season,

So, trust the vibe you get within!

That will lead you to the win!

21

RAY OF HOPE

(James Safo)

The ray of hope that you can feel,

Success is written in your destiny for real,

Tap on the same and go with your heart,

That will be your bright start.

To get that freedom from the blue,

Success is right there waiting for you,

So, embrace it with the feeling all new,

You have to make a choice in few!

The courage to achieve will take you far,

A will to reach your goals for sure,

It's a journey which will teach you a lot,

The most of all the positive thoughts.

Success will motivate you to do better in life,

So, what if you are finding ways to survive,

Keep you hope and you will reach there,

The road of success is sweet and bare.

22

FORGET THE PAST PAIN.

(James Safo)

Celebrate the time and do not worry about tomorrow,
There is happiness in your stride so forget the sorrow,
Value the time you have and its now,
You will love the way and how.

For success comes to those who do things in a positive
way,
Prove your point and have your say,
You will enjoy it through,
Feeling all glee and new!

There is no way for negative thoughts in mind,
Be a little wise and be a little more kind,
And success will be yours for sure,
The feeling so awesome and pure!

Know the value of time and you shall win,
Know what you really want from within,
For your wishes will take you closer to success,
Success that you desire and is yours.

For being successful, you shall smile,
For your every way and every while,

See what reflects comes your way,

See what truly comes today.

Success has its share of difficulties in life,

But amidst all the struggle and strive,

It makes you what you want to be,

It gives you many things to see.

Real success comes with being content,

You know the worth of each penny spent,

It is the ray, which will take you far,

All the best for your endeavors!

23

FLAME OF HOPE

(James Safo)

Like the waves on the shores,

There's always more to explore,

It is unfinished story where we are the writers,

We just got to hold on to our goals tighter.

Don't ever let the flame of hope out in your life,

Without having to strive.

Life is a journey where people come your way,

It doesn't mean that only the good ones are here to

stay.

So, don't be sad if you find bad,

People surrounding you all the time,

Simply set an example for them to be good,

And soon they will mime.

Beauty and peace is what I fear,

Hatred is what my heart adheres,

Life has made me bitter as gall,

I don't give a damn even if I fall.

24

SUCCESS

(James Safo)

All I want to do is reach to the top,

Whoever comes my way I shall drop,

Successful is what I am going to be,

For that I can do anything I need.

Success is both a blessing and a curse,

Success can be for the better or the worse,

You got to be strong,

Or, you'll end up using success to do the wrong.

Success is when you strive for what you want,

When you have that guts to flaunt

Not thinking about the world and wise,

When you can alone suffice.

With your right will and determination,

Where finally you reach your destination,

Real success is hard to find,

But it's one of a kind!

You know you can be successful,

If you have the guts in life,

You know you can reach so far,

If your look is towards the star.

You will reach your goal,
If you know what your role is,
So, all the best for the path,
Destination is near, look at it!

25

THERE IS A NEW DAWN

(James Safo)

If you keep that hope in your heart,

You will get through a perfect start,

Just keep your hope going strong,

You will surely know where you belong.

When it gets all dark outside,

And you just wish you could stay at home and hide,

A silver lining suddenly forms around the cloud,

And almost immediately the quite turns into loud.

The sun peeks right,

It is the most beautiful sight,

Through and the rainbow makes its entrance,

It is the perfect time for romance.

While the darkness is nowhere,

It is taken over by light and the earth is smiling in the air.

For no darkness is here to stay forever,

Eventually light will surely arrive, however.

Life often teaches us new lessons each day,

Some are sweet and some are bitter that way,

But we need to keep going with our gut feeling,

There is so escape or reeling.

If hope is alive then we will stay strong,

Then life would be like an awesome song,

Love is suddenly back in the air,

It is smiling through heaven with pride and flare.

Hope gets you out of the bad,

Makes you happy when you are sad,

Hope gets you out of the pain,

It gives that pleasure in the gain.

26

WHO DID JESUS SAID HE WAS ON EARTH
(James Safo)

Jesus Christ,

Born by virgin Mary,

Jesus who are you?

I am God's leave.

Who are you Jesus?

I am God message.

Honestly who are you?

I am God prophet.

Exactly who are you Jesus?

I am the mesial.

Who are you really?

 I am the son of God,

Come on who are you?

I am son of David.

Truthfully who are you?

I am the son of Abraham.

27

JESUS, PROOF WHO YOU ARE?

(James Safo)

Jesus prove that you are the son of God.

5000 fed with five small loaf of bread and two fish,

turned water into wine,

made cripple walked,

healed the sick,

blind and see,

deaf and hear,

debt were raised,

calmed the sea,

walk on the sea

cure leprosy,

cure infirmity,

thought the gospel up,

Gave salvation uphold God's 10 Commandments,

betrayed by Judas Iscariot,

given 40 stripes,

crucified on the cross,

washed away human sin,

 resurrected after three days,

40 days on earth after resurrection,

Ascended to heaven.

48

Truly Jesus you are the son of God, as especially
messenger of God.

28.

The Voice will go Silent.
(James Safo)

From the mountains, down to the valleys,
To the villages, every street, all alleys,
To every language, kindred tribe and nation,
Goes the call, repentance are words of caution.

The voice growing soar, the message still clear,
Abandon them now, this is Lord's year,
Evil ways leading, to destruction and lost,
Eternally gone, boundary eternally crossed.

The voice is wearing out, come oh my kids,
The safe side with Lord, take his free bids,
Glory here short lived, focus on better things,
The warning still sound, the bell still rings.

The voice is diminishing, urge to open your ear,
The voice will go silent, when no more you shall hear
That time of trouble, such as world not seen,
The destruction shall come, the end of sin.

29.

When the Trumpets Sound

(James Safo)

The sound of the trumpet, a warning of war!

A call for communion too, the voice now soar,

Come let us commune, we prepare for times,

Living in dangerous times, increasing crimes.

Come to the camp, hear the word of the Lord,

Guidelines of this life, that your life be not cold,

Reproves as well, that you live righteous,

For times are coming, times of great crisis.

The messengers of the Lord, prepared with word,

Wait for your response, hope trumpet heard,

Come to the assembly, hearken hears for message,

Inspired by Almighty, to offer divine message.

When the trumpets sound, it can be war or peace,

A call for peace is here, soon the time will cease,

Then trumpets of war sound, that time peace will go,

Salvation will be no more, evil beaten a blow.

30.

Sacred Command,

(James Safo)

From the Eastern, all way to Western,

Religions are similar, even those of ancestors,

In teaching one sacred, command of Lord,

To show love to others, society's strong cord.

There are less privileged, forever they will be with us,

Those who lack in materials, even physically disabled,

A duty for us who have, to share without cuss,

Their esteem to raise, for we they are wrongly labelled.

This is the sacred command, treat all as valuable,

For before the eyes of Lord, even bird he is able,

To take show His divine mercy, to express his great
love,

Opportunity granted to humans, sacred command to
love.

31.

    The Seasoning Salt,

      (James Safo)

Oh, you who hear, and live in the light,

Reflect like moon, always shine bright,

For you are the salt, lacking taste be destroyed,

The salt without taste, its value becomes void.

All yea who brag, of the Lord hear,

The salt is seasoning, throughout the year,

Keeping fresh reason, tenets of society,

The sale without taste, one lives out of piety.

All yea of the word, come taste of the salt,

Tell whether it's valuable, or its mere exalt,

For salt that lacks value, is trodden on the ground,

The salt without taste, you won't be crowned,

The words of the Lord, be the salt of the World,

That you may be tamed, and live not like wild,

Giving the taste of life, to others by your side,

The salt without taste, life will soon be dried.

32.

The Word

(James Safo)

The word of the Lord, is liked to a hammer,

That smashes rock hearts, chipping out the dammar,

Also making joints, strengthening one's life.

The word is a hammer, a command that you strife.

The word of the Lord, is liked to a seed,

Small seed in the soil, breaks grow with speed,

To a huge tree witnessed, in the heart progress too,

The word is a seed, in your heart let it too.

The word of the Lord, is likened to fire,

A strong ire that consumers, sins of a liar,

Wickedness swallowed up, leaving no trace,

The word of the lord is fire, your heart to grace.

The word of the Lord, is likened to light,

Shining in dark hearts, making life bright,

Showing the paths, reflected in character,

The word of the Lord is light, good character to register.

This is history/ evidence of how God protect those who
trust, believe and have faith in Him,
How Almighty God protects people and rewards them
for their suffering.

33.

God Protection

(James Safo)

God protected Noah and his family and animals
 Until he emerged to become the father of the
Entire world.

God protected Jacob in the home of his uncle
Laban,
To escape the wrath of Esau, his elder brother
20 years later Jacob emerged with new family,
God named him Israel , the chosen nation.

God protected Joseph from his 17 year to 30 but,
 His slavery and prison became the school
where,
Almighty God prepare him for greatness,
Became Governor of nations.

God protected Moses in a remote desert for forty
years,
But Moses came forth to liberate the Jews people
From Egypt,

God took away Job earthly riches,
 But protected him for over seven years,
And became richer physically and,
 Spiritually than what he had.

God protected young David,
 To defeat the Philistine giant,
And the philistine fled,
 To set the Israelite free.

God protected Naomi in the barren land of
Moab,
Until she became bitter, she and her daughter in
law,
 Ruth travelled to Bethlehem to participate in,
One of the greatest love stories of history.

God protected David for 15 years,
After he had been anointed King of Israel,
When David finally assumed the throne,
A man of God's own heart,
 And he gave us many of the Psalms.

God protected Elijah,
 By the book Cherith and,

He stood alone against the,
Prophets of Baal on Mount Carmel.

God protected Jonah for three days and,
Three nights in the belly of the whale,
When the protected was over, Jonah went,
To Nineveh and preached history's greatest
revival.

God protected Daniel for 70 years in Babylon,
Where he wrote this old testament book,
Bearing his name outlining the future,
Of God's dealings with his people.

Almighty God protected Esther,
While in the palace of the Persian King,
After three days and night fasting,
She saved her people from destruction.

God protected the disciples,
In the upper room for ten days,
Until the Holy spirit descended in,
To nourished and fashion the church.

God protected Paul,

In the Arabian Desert for 3 years,

And when he came back,

He turned the world upside down.

God protected Paul in a Roman prison,

 And by the time the apostle was free,

 He had written the prison epistles.

 Ephesians, Philippians, Colossians and

Philemon

God protected the apostle John,

 On the Isle of Patmos and the book of revelation,

 The greatest prophetic document of all time,

Was given to all mankind.

.

God protected Jesus in the tomb for 3 days,

 And on the third day,

 Jesus came forth in power,

 To bring salvation to the whole world.

God protected Prophet Muhammad

With spider web at cave entrance,

Fled to safety from persecutors,

God reveal the Quran content.

God Protected James Safo,

From attempted murder and injustice,

Wrote the greatest books on all faiths,

And cornerstone of Faith unity and world peace.

34.

Crown the King

(James Safo)

He sits in the sides of the North,

His Throne angels have set forth,

Chariots of fire be His wheels,

Crown Him Lord of all.

His Glory our eyes can't behold,

For sin bars us from him behold,

Our eyes would be blinded,

Seen His face when tainted.

Crown the King of Mercy,

Forgiving all unlike mercy,

Slow to anger forgiving all,

Holding them up that fall.

Crown the Lord of Grace,

Pure compassion each case,

Loathing sin and hard heart,

Despisers He shall set apart.

35.

The Greatest Wonder!

(James Safo)

There are wonders of the world,

The wall, Machu, world wowed,

But the wonder of wonders,

The Great Lord loves me.

There are billions of stars,

Billions humans are ours,

All known by the maker,

He vows be my caretaker.

The universe in Him coexist,

Held by the might of his fist,

He knows the number of my airs,

The Greatest wonder he cares.

Celebrate in the Great wonder,

The Love of Lord does not wander,

From His wings exposing self,

Like chicks to the danger eagle.

36.

Our God of Light
(James Safo)

The lamp to feet is your word,

Piercing sins in hearts hard,

Herein showcasing your Grace,

Steps to follow for each case.

Since long time through all ages,

We rebelled long history in pages,

Your grace manifested so gently,

By prophets sages speaking eagerly.

Passing the test of time, the word,

Still reveal sinful hearts your herd,

Calling mortals seeking healing,

Compassion in word revealing.

To the world your summons,

Read widely now common,

Myriad of tongues guided,

To life of light and joy.

37.

The King is Coming.

(James Safo)

He shall appear when morning dawns,

When light triumphantly on hills shines,

Upon hills of East gilding beauty,

Awaking life's joy a final cutie.

Brighter than the rising moon even sun,

Vanquishing the pain experienced gun,

Light dawning upon all generations,

The day of marvelous splendor on nations.

Accompanied by a Mighty army of angels,

Lightning striking do dim our sun for ages,

Grandeur never seen before on our skies,

All glory to wipe away all people's cries.

The King shall come in that morning,

He shall not hesitate even in mourning,

The call is now extended come refuse not,

Join the glory of the King so he rejects you not.

38.

Nothing is Worth

(James Safo)

What shall stand between me and Lord,

Delusiveness of the world or the sword,

I renounce the attractiveness of sin,

Surrendering to only certain way to win.

Habits of life and pleasures of lust,

To many appear harmless losing trust,

But they tear relationships apart,

The good Lord's protection depart.

Let nothing from Him my heart sever,

It's now worth losing everlasting forever,

For all this is for but a limited period,

Clinging to the Almighty blessings myriad.

Even the hardest of my trials,

Even the world against smiles,

Always to the Lord in prayer,

For nothing is worthy my Lord.

39.

My Life I Surrender.

(James Safo)

My whole life to you I surrender,

My hands to you my defender,

Guide them according to your will,

Moving at the impulse of your love.

My lips too fill with your message,

That they may be channel passage,

My gold silver and all wealth,

Nothing is mine till my death.

My feet oh Lord give speed,

To walk your ways as freed,

Let me sing always for my king,

Dwell in your kingdom to bring.

My love I surrender to you,

That wisdom may accrue,

To live righteously here,

And join you in life after.

40.

Rock or Sinking Sand.

(James Safo)

Standing on the solid Rock Christ,

The wisdom of heaven priced,

The call to build on the rock,

The waves can't weaken block.

The sinking sand you warned,

That foolishness you informed,

The waves shall come strong,

And destruction shall belong.

The things of world sinking sand,

Like dew life passes unplanned,

All hoarded becomes meaningless,

The sinking sand epitome foolishness.

The solid Rock sends invites,

That you may live in city lights,

The rock gives certainty of hope,

Choose ye the solid Rock.

41.

The Sun Shines Forever.

(James Safo)

In the city far away,

Naked eyes see no ray,

There is no night there,

Light there passes in glare.

The pearly gates we enter,

The golden streets tender,

The dazzling light we see,

The Sun will shine forever.

The melodious angels will sing,

Chirping tunes for the King,

Humans welcoming home at last,

To partake in the joy and blast.

The Gates will be open forever,

The call to enter not be ever,

Now the call to register a member,

For the Sun will shine Glory forever.

42.
    He's always there for me
        (James Safo)

Sometime the world comes crushing,
Chaos almost crumble me,
But I turn my heart onto you Almighty,
Always full of grace and glory.

Oh! my dear master,
You lift me out of my troubles
Always standing by my side,
Comforting my pains.

In my deepest moments,
I call onto you my dearest one
You listen to my prayers,
Never goes unanswered my plea.

My all-time companion,
My loyalty unto you I pledge,
In times of joy and bliss,
You never abandon me,
In you I will dwell forever.

43.

I will get through

(James Safo)

Dear lord, my troubles,

Are huge and grave-like,

I fail to understand what to do,

I would pay dearly,

For my wickedness and sinfulness.

My world almost crumbling,

No place safe for me,

My right is wrong,

My wrong is right,

Help me lord to discover,

Your rightful ways.

Dear lord in you I believe,

That all will be well,

You gonna help me to overcome,

At last you will assure me,

An everlasting life in heaven.

44.

Protect me from myself

(James Safo)

My holy most heavenly father,

Save me from myself,

My ever-ending needs,

Always wanting some more.

I am wicked and proud,

My selfishness leading me,

To always want the best before the others,

Protect me dear father,

My strong ambitions and desires almost destroying me.

You are a faithful and famous God,

Save me from the world,

Always pulling me to the worldly pleasures,

Bring me to your eternity,

Let me dwell in your paradise.

In humility in my human nature,

I give my life to you,

In faith you promise me,

That every desire you fulfil,

Save me dear lord, your wicked servant.

45.

My son
(James Safo)

It feels very guilty to see you son abandon the
light,
Despite my tireless time teaching you the right,
Leading by example in worship and prayer,
Now you turn to be darkness at daytime with little
care.

I know these words hits you right onto your face,
Why do you exit from the lord and vow not
embrace?
Son, his existence you now question, and you
have denied,
The truth and faith I have taught you since birth
you now set aside.

Be keen because the life lesson must be learned,
In the due course, God may be furious, and you
will get spurned,
The scripture has it that his words never get back
void,
Even when Satan's tactics are tactfully deployed.

Dear son have faith and you will fair,

Valleys of darkness and tears you will not toe,

His grace is marvellous, and his will be always be
done,

Hold onto your faith and he will show you the
light,

In him you will reign forever without flight.

46.

The gift of faith
(James Safo)

It does not come from man's years of striven,
It is not conjured up, but it is freely given.
Faith the most paramount gift to believes driven,
Sinners left struggling, cursing and fallen.

God's scriptures to man speak of it,
Though a willing and righteous heart receive it,
It is a marvellous gift that sets all men free of
temptations,
Filling them with everlasting peace for all happy
nations.

The wicked and sinful man fails to acknowledge,
God's , singing his grace,
Very few understand his great salvation story.
With it trials we overcome in God's assistance,
Sinners and those of little faith remain with their
resistance.

It comes from the holy spirit,
A gift good people of grace merit,

Our dear Lords has good plans for us but seeks
for our compliance,
Together in faith we will walk the path of
righteousness in alliance.

47.

In faith by faith through faith

(James Safo)

Through faith we get to know,

Things beyond our human understanding,

Our beloved God's own work pattern,

In that manner every threat we learn.

By faith we all understand,

Tracing our pathways and life stand,

By faith we remain remnants of grace bound with

his golden strand,

Even when temptations threaten to expand,

By faith we remain loyal to him.

Through faith, we all understand his ways,

Even when our short sight becomes dim,

His love remains in our hearts grim,

Through faith, we know the way,

Our sinful hearts obey.

48.

He's my light

(James Safo)

God is my light, guiding me through darkness of
day,

He never leads me astray,

Anytime troubles get near,

I worry not for he will make the paths clear.

He is my light and strength,

every single molecule of breath,

in him my faith has increased in length,

I dive in deep oceans full tides of life,

In him, I remain strong despite all the strife.

He lets my candle continue to burn,

I illuminate the lives of others so my footsteps
they learn,

He never lets me shadow his flame,

For I always work in his ways and name.

49.

He will get me through

  (James Safo)

He will get me through as I walk into this life journey,
He will comfort me in all stress and distress, pulling me
astray,
He will lighten my paths like array,
He will give me a gift direction so will have nothing to
guess.

Even if I falter on the filthy way so rough,
And the ground grown rough and tough,
When all my burdens bundles intensely,
He will restore my hope and move me from
the hoop.

During my cold hour, our cry so loud,
When I am in a hostile surrounding with
 crowd, Against me,
When every step I make seem dominated and,
Dominated with/by pain,
 All turning mean and meaningless gone,
In him I a cast my tribulations and trial for he, Helps me
start again.

50.

God is not breaking me
(James Safo)
I live on the crust and trust in him,
For he is not breaking me but making me.
In me he is fulfilling his plan,
For the world and is messing my span.

He is giving me moments even if the darkness
surround me,
Making my vane valleys a soft place for me to
dwell,
He is teaching and training me well,
Even under the triumphs so cruel,
In him am sure it will be well.

Even though at times my faith falter,
Feeling to fight my own battle,
At times I feel deserted desert,
Without oasis or horses to assert,
My hope for tomorrow.

At these times I feel fatigued and all becomes
futile,
My efforts appearing apelike and time stands still,
Hopelessly am left helpless,
But I know dear lord is not breaking me.
51.

Let me be like you

(James Safo)

Oh! dear lord let me know your way,

Let me know what to do today,

You show me how to pray,

But I feel like way that is the only holy will.

Dear lord help me through the hazardous world,

Full of perverted priorities so painful like a wound,

Dear Father, direct my mind to the right direction,

Let my formless life focus onto your assertion.

Dear lord onto you I profess my faith,

For you fill my life with everlasting love,

Let me assist the assailants be like dove,

So, all of us can be like you in words

and deeds.

VICTORY

TOTAL
Victory
Obtaining victory through prayers
IMPACT
GOSPEL

52.

VICTORY Poems

WE ARE VICTORS

(James Safo)

The days of darkness are over,

light is here at last,

The cold nights of fear and terror,

Disappeared with the   moon,

Nights raged by the devil,

where no one could withstand.

The shield wall is broken,

Alone stands the meanest defense,

Disease surely, almost took me into the

other world,

Could have been a curse,

Curses of the demons and sadists,

At last, I can heave a relief,

there is no pain, full health assured.

53.

DON'T GIVE UP

(James Safo)

Victors are overcomers, those who choose not to give
up,
These have wages in full portions,
they fight a good fight, victory begets them,
I learnt that life is no consequential,
Curses only exist amongst the non-believers.

At last, I stand still; I defy falling at all,
I could be departed by now,
but I chose to have hope for life,
I am a living testimony,
that with hope we live to tell a story.

54.

BANQUET OF VICTORY

(James Safo)

The strong walls of the castles had sunk,

No longer stood as it had for decades,

The beautiful scenery surrounding the castle,

Was filled with withered flowers and dust.

All the captains are taking by the shores,

Ready to troll the ship to the promised land,

Sitting beside are jubilant villagers,

All with raided glad and exulting noises.

Moving towards their ancestral land,

A land that gave them birth,

Memoirs of row and mourn fresh in their minds,

how they were evicted, and their houses brought down,

Women cannot hide their joy,

They beating their breasts and making ululations in

Ecstasy,

Men whistle during this feast of joy,

All proud of their victory.

55.

DIED TOO EARLY

(James Safo)

So unlucky are the dead,

"Fare thee well" you did not live to see the fruits of our

labour,

A decade of fighting characterized with bloodshed,

Could not watch as our treasured land taken by

Merciless settlers,

Now the jade fight is over,

Hopefully never again to recur.

All of us, who's homewards were destroyed,

Are now heaving a sigh of relief,

Many lost hopes other fall by stroke,

Could not imagine their lifetime investments take away,

United as a people we have stood,

At last, we are walking to our ancestry.

56.

Strong woman-Kiahna

(By James Safo)

On Your Wings Mary,

What a joy to see you daughter in your cap and tassel,

You are now set to pull the world to your castle,

Just the other day you were a little girl,

Watched everything you did and was sure,

That one day you will be daddy's treasure.

Now am watching you Kiahna graduate,

A responsible and a very strong lady I helped create,

For sure on the wings of knowledge you fly,

Always follow your vision and your star will rise high.

It took you perseverance and hard work Kiki,

Driven by your great urge for success,

Your self-opinion and determination is today confess,

Today Kiki, daddy's girls you master the academic dance,

You have indeed utilized your one life and chance

I knew you'll do it right.

At twenty-one you have worked hard to get a bachelors,

Safo's have now a new psychologist in the house,

We are convinced that you'll fulfil your dreams,

 within you are the qualities it deems,

Congratulations graduate.

57.

HE MADE IMPOSSIBLE, POSSIBLE.

(By James Safo)

He is sparkles of sunshine,

Shimmering stars studding serene sunsets,

Elliot,

He reminds me every day that children are a heritage,

Our strength and breath in all age,

The new generation change,

And free birds not in a cage.

He possess an amazing personality,

His rich acts, speech and responsibility,

He is incredibly intelligent,

He is my heir, the air I breathe frequent,

He is quiet knowledgeable, knotless and divergent,

He is immensely talented,

He is my son, my world class sport undisputed.

 May have missed a few parent teacher conferences,

Not been there to solve their tough trigonometric,

But God stood there amphitheatric.

His accolades go beyond,

Great victory they correspond,

My all-time flower and flour

in our kitchen,

Oh, he owes the best universities,

And that scholarship proves his unmatched qualities,

It took days of immaculate and immeasurable sacrifice,

Long nights up studying neat with counterbalance.

His successes are highly remarkable,

Brain of Britain unchallengeable,

Twice a twinflower,

Sterling A* star in his GCSE's,

and Advanced level A's,

his sportsmanship spotted you break barriers,

Seen him lead his peer athletes scene for five years
frontiers,

His first High Jump hail at Harvard,

93-year-old record henceforward,

And he did not stopped at that,

Gold medallist: Olympics, Commonwealth, Europe, UK,
England,

Bronze medallist made him the world reflect like an icon
scope,

And also a 100-metre sprinter,

Besides an Educational spot and sports trouble-
shooter,

His siblings, parent particularly,

and thousands of fans throughout the globe

are proud for his probe.

And stand straight to salute him (Elliot Safo),

He makes impossible possible

That makes him historically one in a billion in the world.

The constant favour has continued to be with him,

His determination earning him degree in Finance and Economics acclaim,

His empowerment leading to employment in banking and finance reclaim,

 His strain earning great grapelike strides to a greater destiny Antrim.

As a withstanding winner

Always.

58.

SLAVE OF GOD.

(James Safo)

My story is nothing short of remarkable,

But what is life less ups and downs,

It is a harrowing and narrow narrative full of frowns,

 It deems high, demands to be told.

What would you serve to survive?.

No single hunk only hunger,

Pauperism poverty hypersensitive,

In a desperate desolate,

And a loner.

An abandoned child chilling like an old owl,

Abandoned and straddling in the streets,

 Competing with dogs for scraps,

 Of food in the gutters of Ghana,

A turnaround narrative,

To one of Europe's richest, most successful

 Businessman.

Wealth became fun, fancy and nice,

Making friends and foes,

Abruptly toughness on toes,

Fear and failure arose,

Plights and Plots to fall me,

And then it happened.

A miscarriage of justice stripped everything,

Left me bare,

With nothing to bear,

Other than my faith in here (heart).

Every cloud has a silver lining,

Rose again to more than twice I had,

 World leader; leading author and publisher,

LLM(Master of Laws) BA (Hons; Law and account,

A Master's degree; international laws, Business CRS,

Human Right, Legal research, institutional development

and management,

Certificate in Education,

Cert in Accounting,

psy.N, G.N, (Nursing),

Diploma in Criminology and crime detection,

Diploma in broadcast media (Auto & Bio, tv, radio and

film),

Diploma in (H & S),

Certificate in Business,

Microsoft specialist.

Dip in photography and computer.

My story is a story of grace,

My tried life is told off my face,

From scraps of fussy food to chase,

To greatness I rose.

When I look back at my jobless journey,

I believe that God the shaper shaped it like winey,

From revering experiences and ravaging hunger,

Remade struggle for remains of a burger,

To London, a freezer.

A journey that saw me rise,

A quarter a century amass

International colleges,

Care homes,

Letting agencies,

Law firms,

Among other businesses,

On a single dawn brought down to ashes,

Left me bear with nothing to bear,

Other than my faith in here (heart).

There God found me,

Reminded me,

Job and Joseph,

Saved slaves of the Almighty,

And so I would be too,

James.

And from my wicked and weakest,

Over 30 books I wrote published,

E-booked and paper backed,

Translated,

English to French, Chinese, Arabic, Spanish translated,

Between average 450 pages each,

The near future holds,

Five more books,

The testimony attests,

Miracles,

Blessings,

God's capabilities.

It's my predisposition to preach faith,

Unity and truth,

To the whole world faith,

In God Almighty/ Allah is their faith,

Justice for Judgement is close by,

Prepare do, procrastinate don't buy,

From sunrise repent all and sundry,

My Mission word is to unite the world religious faith,

To forgive, forget and to love,

To have firm faith and to believe,

That the almighty God/ Allah/ Parama Namba,

Is the key to God's kingdom.

For heaven is our home,

Not the earth and fake fame,

In all humility and not humour seek Him,

Know him.

59.

A WALK OF SUCCESS
    (James Safo)

The whole school marched in procession, with
happiness and gratification.
Before the students were the city bands, with
guitars, drums and trumpets.
With neat navy blues suits, white shirts and
maroon stripped ties,
All adding to their flair looks.
Boys and girls in two lines all sung praises,
holding their school flag high.

The passer-by(s) stood flabbergasted, thought
the president was coming in town,
Each face portrayed a flamboyant smile, a sign of
victory and satisfaction,
The songs filled the air and the schools buses
hooted rhythmically,
The spirit of success failed everyone; the
candidates had made history.

Indeed, it was a new dawn; the last year's,
candidates had broken the record.

Appeared in local newspapers and international
news,
  Indeed placed our school on the world map,
They had proven a nation's strength in promoting
an education,
No wonder the president in his routine briefing,
had mentioned the school.

Success is a fruit of hard work,
The proverb saying says hard work pays.
Alarm clocks were set for dawn studies,
  Other burnt midnight fuel in studies,
Mathematics and science well performed,
Teachers had to also joining the victory march.
Forever shall our flag fly; we vow to keep the
record.

LIFE IS VICTORY

(James Safo)

Life is story-holding dreams entire,

Life strengthens hopes makes them true desire,

Life is nothing but a process higher,

Life is good if your smoke lights fire.

Life is an achievement like a wind-lot by,

Life is a competition the limit is the sky,

Life is way beyond the sky set your goals high,

Life full of fulfilment is merry close to fly.

Life is made of wings to flight,

Everyone endowed with their capacity to fight,

A life blossoming is success is bright,

Glorifying and a gratifying in sight.

What a contented heart almost to sublime,

Makes a gold-worth prime,

Victory reigns in clime,

Always hails joy loud like chime.

61.

IF YOU THINK

(James Safo)

If you think you can, you can,

If you think you can't, you can't,

If you think you'll lose, you will,

If you think not to dare, you don't.

If you feel like you need not to try,

If you try, you lose,

For it, all begins with your mindset,

Victory begins not from without,

For the victors have set their mind.

If you think you don't belong, you don't,

Oh my dearest think, think about what you think,

If your is success beware to think about it,.

If you think of standing, then rise.

For life is an ocean, swim to your island,

Life is a battle, fight for your position,

Oh dear ones,

If you want, you have to think,

A man who thinks he can, does,

For a man who think he can't, Can't.

WHAT IS SUCCESS?
(James Safo)

Success is the power and synergy,

The ability to emerge after pedagogy,

From your friends you receive porgy,

Everyone acknowledges your energy.

Success is might and ability to suppress,

It is not the prevail over regress,

Success is not a crown for mess,

Success like a recess,

Comes over a period of apsis.

Success is not for fame,

But a feeling of beating the lame,

When you succeed, you defame,

The self-proclaimed non-tame.

63.

IT'S TIME TO FLY

(James Safo)

"It is time, time to leave the nest and take your

wings",

Said the mother-bird,

It is due time, your time to fly,

I am convinced that you can,

I have given you the necessary mantra for takeover.

You must be sure of your ability,

Be sure to emerge successful,

Deep within me I am optimistic,

That dear son you will succeed.

64.

THE SKY IS NOT YOUR LIMIT.

(James Safo)

The sun and stars are also a possibility,
My beloved son if you didn't know this,
You were born to succeed,
To fly…fly…fly without perching.

Oh my little bird,
Challenge the impossibilities,
Be ready to explore,
Be ready face life alone.

65.

VICTORS AREN'T PESSIMISTS.

(James Safo)

After long period of trial you are gifted with

victory,

What happiness comes with success,

For having a fulfilling life.

Not the length of life you live but the live for the

days you live.

Victory sees no pessimists,

Those are too lazy to attempt,

Too proud to stomach the feelings of failure,

For victors are come from series of failures.

A true victor is one who makes,

An indelible mark without smearing others,

A victor always moves informed by the pursuit of

their desires,

A victors is one who makes work their friend.

A victor is always goal oriented,

Avery time prepared for take-off,

Never discouraged by roughness along the way,

A victor is at every time positive,

Always affirmative to move through the rough

course.

8

66.

JOURNEY TO SUCCESS

(James Safo)

Everyone wants to success in their endeavours,

But few people look at the path to success.

Success does not come to the perfectionists,

Those who are very scared of losing and dare not

try.

Success is taking courage,

Daring to do even when you have little hope to

succeed.

Working with your full potential

Not listening to the pessimists and negative

energies.

Success is being positive,

Always hoping to aspire and emerge victorious.

Success requires one to live their life with own

parameters,

Not always comparing your achievement with

others.

Success requires you to be proud,

For reaching beyond what you thought in the first

place.

Success is beating all our obstacles,

Attaining our achievements however minor they

may appear.

WHO SAYS YOU CAN'T?

(James Safo)

Leave the doubting Thomas alone,

They will also question your ability.

They always say things cannot be done,

And that most things on are impossible,

But tell them everything under the sun is

possible.

They are always filled with negativity,

But to listen to them is a second stupidity,

Be wise and work with determination,

Go in full swing till you succeed.

Be sure to walk with perseverance,

For failure brings arrogance.

Continue toiling to avoid failures,

Success bring everlasting joy in abundance.

68.

PATIENTS BEGETS SUCCESS,
(James Safo)

Success does not come overnight,
It is a result of continued insight.
Success requires one to deploy full potential,
Always being hopeful and resilient.

Success is striving for the best,
Success is seldom looking to the right or left,
But remaining focused on the course.
Success is working with the successful,
Having the patience through the times of storm
and stress.

Success is seeing beyond our dark days,
Remaining focused to the island.
Successful people remain awake overnight,
When the others have grown tired and went to
slumber.

69.

IMAGINATION

(James Safo)

Imagination is the beginning of creation,

 You imagine what you want;

you desire what you imagine;

and finally, you create what you want,

 So everything comes from us,

 and only we are capable of great things.

70.

TASTE OF SWEETNESS.

(James Safo)

The journey had been long,

The quest for self-determination,

The struggle of guns & bombs,

To reclaim from colonialists, lost.

The struggle was vicious,

The battles in the forests,

The detentions in prisons,

The torture in our land.

The slavery had been long,

Burned with long working hours,

Paid nuts to till our land,

Benefitting foreigners, usurpers.

The victory is welcomed,

Colonialists kicked out,

Self-determination is welcome,

Freedom in our land.

71.

HOME AT LAST
(James Safo)

The long stint, burdensome,

In foreign world, add to sum,

Hunger struck, diseases biting,

Long a stint, home now hitting.

To reclaim the rock, rebuilt nation,

Broken by war, its children donation,

To foreign worlds given, save haven,

Long a stint, home now hitting.

Beaten by the fangs of refugee status,

No education, scanty food, poor sanitation,

Yet unbroken, though situation biting,

Long a stint, home now hitting.

The journey is long, lighter than foreign stint,

Bundled in lorries, joyful songs, ringing air,

Final journey home, refugee status abandoned,

Long a sting, home now hitting.

72.

THE SONG OF VICTORS.
(James Safo)

Teenage life wholly spent, chasing basics,

In education system, chasing the crown,

Under instructions, many years waiting,

In anticipation, joyful conclusion foreseeing.

Intensive system, rigorous curriculum that,

Many partakers quit, tactics elsewhere seeking,

Perseverance a virtue, mandatory so conclude,

The joy of victors, near future foreseeing.

Final tests mandatory, preparation next step,

New energy mandatory, final lap breath,

Held but for victory, coming to hard workers,

Working and reworking, all formulas mastering.

The long wait, as states holds destiny,

Time slows down, but all work completed,

Finally, the news breaking, breathe withheld,

Jubilations all over, for work of victors rewarded.

73.

THE KEYS AT HAND
(James Safo)

The key to success, motto inscribed,
Speaking broadly, educations' importance,
Beseeching focus, strict adherence to vision,
Retelling again and again, the keys at hand.

The atmosphere sober, well-seasoned for studies,
Resources availed much, focus emphasized daily,
Discipline religiously demanded, of studies as well,
Working nation's future, handing generations keys.

Churning out experts, annual mandate given,
Instructing future success, nation's destiny creating,
Capacity growing daily, corporates indirectly staffing,
Working nation's future, handing generations keys.

Annual celebrations, yearly success evident.
The keys to success, yet again handed over,
Powers to excel, handed over to generation,
Positioned to succeed, victors receive the keys.

74..

NO SURRENDER.

(James Safo)

Deep in the village, arrangements are ripe,

Older than her father, cause if the hype,

Cows and goats given, minds finally lost,

Bound by deadly culture, bright destiny lost.

She is torn, loving parents and pursuing goal,

The Gospel preached, quitting is digging hole,

Determined to bring change, tied by poverty,

Parents' life to change, acquisition of real property.

It's time to flee, further delay is deadly,

A rescue center, miles away only hope,

Walking in deep night, wild animals roaring,

Daring to pursue, better life promised.

Years of hot pursuit, sickening anger of father,

Wealth retrieved, once bride eloped,

The Hero has conquered, academically excellent.

Returns a hero, role model to generations.

75.

THE SONG OF VICTORS.

(James Safo)

Teenage life wholly spent, chasing basics,

In education system, chasing the crown,

Under instructions, many years waiting,

In anticipation, joyful conclusion foreseeing.

Intensive system, rigorous curriculum that,

Many partakers quit, tactics elsewhere seeking,

Perseverance a virtue, mandatory so conclude,

The joy of victors, near future foreseeing.

Final tests mandatory, preparation next step,

New energy mandatory, final lap breath,

Held but for victory, coming to hard workers,

Working and reworking, all formulas mastering.

The long wait, as states holds destiny,

Time slows down, but all work completed,

Finally, the news breaking, breathe withheld,

Jubilations all over, for work of victors rewarded.

76.

THE KEYS AT HAND
(James Safo)

The key to success, motto inscribed,
Speaking broadly, educations' importance,
Beseeching focus, strict adherence to vision,
Retelling again and again, the keys at hand.

The atmosphere sober, well-seasoned for studies,
Resources availed much, focus emphasized daily,
Discipline religiously demanded, of studies as well,
Working nation's future, handing generations keys.

Churning out experts, annual mandate given,
Instructing future success, nation's destiny creating,
Capacity growing daily, corporates indirectly staffing,
Working nation's future, handing generations keys.

Annual celebrations, yearly success evident.
The keys to success, yet again handed over,
Powers to excel, handed over to generation,
Positioned to succeed, victors receive the keys.

77.

NO LONGER A SLAVE
(James Safo)

It was a simple out, business invitation,
Discussing partnership, venue complication,
Friends cum foes, introducing liquor,
First taste second, end drinking spree.

Days of gloom, dependency spelling doom,
Hoping from party, dosage like drug,
Spending the last, earnings depleted days,
No longer performing, without daily drug.

The toll is strong, rescue mission needed,
To shake off effects, regain strength,
Spirited fight this, locked with doctor,
Days of seclusion, denial unlike actor.

The stint finally, ends with declaration,
Battle well fought, victory finally achieved,
Dependency at last, taste smell loathing,
No longer slave, of drugs dependency.

78.

THE SPLASH

(James Safo)

The Pool was cool, the breeze light,

Small waves here, unidentified plight,

Of people living, knowing poor peace,

Small waves return, periodic but cease.

The prior period, volatile due politics,

Threatening pool, stability of bricks,

Then day victory, turned sour news,

Huge stone cast, shocking casing fusing.

Once small waves, now splashes 'where,

Blood gushing out, bodies lying bare,

Blood bath here, pain of bad politics,

People once peace, fight each other.

The truce mandatory, pool' safety guarantee,

People come together; peace must be.

Leaders forging unity, saving country rocked,

Pool peace restored, people back celebrating.

79.

LET PEOPLE GO.
(James Safo)

The songs of war, in mountains valleys,
Dominion must end, ringing streets alleys,
Demand for end, long overdue freedom,
State capture seen, few claiming infallible.

Crying for emancipation, songs of freedom,
Hopes of change, creating equity kingdom,
Let people go, chains strength weak,
Bondage is over, others time speak.

Dynasties time out, pave way democracy,
Let people decide, key tenet democracy,
Chains poverty break, vision new heights,
Meet think together, exercising their rights.

Let people go, song heard across,
Valleys alleys villages, across same rhythm,
In numbers celebrating, victory over dynasty,
Future generations reminded, Let people go.

80.

PHASE IT OUT.

(James Safo)

Long time ago, soldiers stood up,

Fighting without fear, evils in society

Profiling on race, favour in cup,

Threatening unity, people in anxiety.

Street walks everywhere, demanding equal rights,

People of colour, inequalities times resisting,

Quietly and loudly, peacefully showing plight,

Though met violence, spirited fight putting.

Science proving wrong, theory inferior mind,

History standing guard, all created equal,

Phase it out, cries demands combined,

Allow tired body, equality time resting.

Phase it out, song still sounding,

Decades down line, promised land seeing,

Work, voting, education, light shining bright,

Hope ignited hearts, fighting showing plight.

81.

NO MORE SCARE.

(James Safo)

The close 20th century, burdened with calamities,

Spelling doom next, century of scientific revolution,

Falling by thousands, science giving no cure,

Tearing families apart, grabbing father mother.

Little chances given, all infected doomed,

Their fate sealed, life once plumed,

Efforts from corners, remedy sought much,

Countless studies reported, not availing much.

The century inception, brought scientific break-through,

Medication giving support, sustenance making debut,

Bring hope millions, living positive globally,

Reducing death rate, soon obliterated totally.

Once dark century, now full of light,

Beaming faces there, hope cure bright,

Pandemic consumed soon, victory celebrated much,

No more a scare, the pandemic of century.

82.

The War on the Cut.
(James Safo)

The pain inflicted, innocent girls by culture,
Evil culture long gone, times of modern culture,
To inflict discipline, by cutting the clitoris,
An act endangering life, yet a common chorus.

The cries rang loud, from the rivers in the forests,
The knife of the old lady, no more in the wrists,
Penalties we have imposed, you age no matter,
Keeping you in long jail, your life we will tatter.

Let them keep their nature, as given by their maker,
Your knife is painful, it shall no longer break her,
The cut is meaningless, the state is hunting you,
Be sure to be castrated, to live like the ewe.

The war on the cut, waged even to the deep land,
Policies coming up, the cut in now banned,
Actions have been taken, on all who take pride,
Inflicting pain on her! She will be a natural bride.

83.

This Monster

(James Safo)

They say they saw, light in the end of tunnel,
We lived in darkness, led in poverty channel,
Our necks held tightly, strangling us to death,
The manner of huge snake, prey denying breath.

We cried in the streets, that action may be taken,
All of the leaders, their character embezzle akin,
To fight the monster, all energy was in vain,
Imposing real measures, to system was pain.

Our matching on, was not to be deterred,
By inaction of agents, whose anger we stirred,
The spirit unquenchable, the war to their doors,
Calling them to action, to commence the wars,

Rewarding are the efforts, energy bearing fruits,
We the lie low, whose wealth; corrupt roots,
Celebrating their convictions, jail terms deserved,
Emancipating the people, punishment well served.

84.

The Flushed King.
(James Safo)

Him that ruled, with iron fist,
Ringed everywhere, by fierce men,
Wielding power, none could have a gist,
Enemies like Daniel, dying in lion's den.

He destroyed our land, unemployment high,
Living costs high, all aspects of life awry,
His lieutenants looting, running all down,
A country once rich, all fortune drown.

The uprising people, we demanded change,
An end of tyranny, people moved with rage,
Baying for his blood, flushed out the king,
Like provoked bees, injected with the sting.

Freedom restored, prosperity hopes restored,
New opportunities, wealth ready to hoard,
Systems improving, medical care for all,
Good times ahead, celebration for us all.

85.

The Gladiators War.

(James Safo)

When the bells sounded, fear grasped majority,
Few were determined, to fight the authority,
A cruel regime which, determined to enslave natives,
Getting people work, tilling farms for no incentives,

The teams worked, staging war all direction,
Activism taking the lead, violence an option,
Mission guiding them, colonizers' must leave,
The stay being long, no longer allowed to cleave,

Walking to the forests, armed to teeth,
Heavy fire unleashing, ready to lay wreath,
Enemy of our people, time is here,
The war of Gladiators, fire you hear.

The pressure mounted, yielded victory across,
The continent liberated, to be their own boss,
Celebrations mood ignited, even as they walk away,
Giving back our land, paving the success way.

86.

The Path not Taken.

(James Safo)

They definitely worked hard, the future was all bright,

The enrolment was welcomed, income first bite,

Early days so sweet, learning new tricks,

Rising up the ranks, like builder with bricks.

Continuing the path of light, then worst happened,

Shrinking to terrible losses, termination saddened,

The axe cuts without mercy, times indeed hard,

Time to quit the cities, the fine back yard.

Most sinking to depression, difficulty to cope,

Financial drain setting, families clinging to hope,

Yet he chose to ignite, his desire for business,

Working simple things, food production business.

Years down and expanding, growing timely,

Supplying to chains, product of hard work,

The Path not taken, few agree to embark,

Joy of self-reliance, shines life brightly.

87.

The song of the River.
 (James Safo)

Deep into the rainforests,
Far away from modernity,
In the forgotten dense forests,
Is the story of post-modernity.
Of grave sadness and hope,
A people still unknown,
Torn to levels they can't cope,
Shattered by the bone.

Deep in the dark thickets,
The story of a warrior,
Tending to victims of war,
Singly even without supplies,
Victims of rape story untold,
Saving lives daily his core,
Burden great upon shoulder,
Celebration for life molder.

The song of the long River,
Daily gives energy to Liver,
Amidst the darkness of tress,
Victory daily pain ease.

88.

The Rules of the Game
(James Safo)

The game of the living,
Is founded on strict rules,
One must keep believing,
That failure he can overrule.

Live is for the living,
Their lives always working,
No joy in lazy bones,
Poverty creates zones.

Success comes in ways,
Goals remain focus always,
Deviation is forbidden,
Poison to failure hidden.

The rules of the game,
Mistakes take the blame,
Organize fast a comeback,
Giving up ever last option.

89.

Empty Pockets

(James Safo)

Back in the days of darkness,

When sun beat with harshness,

Back in the forgotten village,

When feet hit the mileage.

There in that crumbling hut,

Poverty struggle much to cut,

Against the odds, she fought,

90.

To crowns that she got.
   (James Safo)

There in the desert sun,

She tended sheep one,

Always fighting in class,

Even tougher than brass.

Now she dines with noble,

Streets of palaces a model,

Holding the nuclear buttons,

Empty pockets abhor gluttons.

91.

Optimism Fire
(James Safo)

We knew her from husband,
Prominent, wisdom abundant,
Cracking the glass ceiling,
Mask of chauvinism pealing.

The girl from the south,
Assured us of her prowess,
Sharp when opens mouth,
Optimism indeed boundless.

Enter the trail in the cities,
Streets alleys smelling victory,
Trust her with our pretties,
Perfect time to write history.
Come the final day,
The numbers thronged,
Celebration long way,
Ceiling glass hit hard.

92.

Desire is the Genesis

(James Safo)

It begins with desire,
To change status quo,
New living to sire,
Re-energizing to grow.

It boils to action,
Steps right direction,
Eyes stayed to goals,
No adjusting the poles.

Then comes strict discipline,
Controlled action one line,
Always avoiding distraction,
Ignoring negative traction.

Desire is the genesis,
Coupled with work,
Guided by discipline,
Recipe to great victory.

93.

Climbing the Mountain.

(James Safo)

The snowy mountain peak,
On a sunny morning bleak,
Scenery indeed picturesque,
Desire to climb atop burning.

The climb of the mountain,
The scenic rivers fountain,
To wind up tough journey,
Demands a trained army.

The climb of the height,
Deprives breathing rights,
Congesting the chest,
Oppressing the breast.

The victory of the climb,
The land above is prime,
The land below inferior,
The climb of the mountain worth.

94.

Keep the Bow Stretched.

(James Safo)

Fired up ready for war,

To fight on you swore,

Try not relent at all,

Misery inviting better crawl

Keep the bow stretched,

Best position is stretched,

Release arrows when due,

Right direction it flew.

Keep the fire burning boy,

Enemies you shall annoy,

For the pleaser of friends,

Will end up with bends.

The sweetness of victory,

A story of bow stretched,

Fire kept burning always,

Deserved victory enjoy.

95.

Never stop to try

(James Safo)

Never get tired of trying,

For victors are victims of failed trials,

If you wish to attain attempted goals,

Never get near to losing hope.

How much do you feel to have strained?

Do you think of those who attained?

Never ever losing hope they learned,

Now they are flowing in glory earned.

You have split spirit deterring your goal,

You need be focused like miners of coal.

At last when you least expect you will sit,

Celebrate, dance victory and like a king you will

eat.

96.

Go for it

(James Safo)

Success like luminous paper eludes people,
People who ponder like poppers,
It is not given on a golden platter,
It is rather achieved by achievers.

It requires redeemed sacrifice,
Working tirelessly as if giving service,
Why fill you mind will unnecessary malice,
To think that victory is served like rice.

Victory begets the vantage who labour,
To them it comes easy like a ship docking on the
harbour,
Eventually they sing in success with tabor,
They have made much so don't belabour.

97.

No tricks to success.

(James Safo)

What is your dearest dream?
How wild are you with your will to succeed?
Don't you have the hope to make the world's
wonders?
To show everyone the sure steps to greatness.

But are you ready on the rear or affront of your
desire?
Are you ready to pay the painful price without
tire?
Learning all lessons lined along your path,
Heeding to heroes advices for they have
advanced and are worth.

There are no guarantees or guardians to give
sure tricks,
But you have to rely on you passion not peer
tracks,
Your strain and strength define your lucks,
Pushes you to your perfect victory gates.

98.

The untold story of every victor.
   (James Safo)
From a black tinted tidy luxurious car emerged a
man,
With a well-built body not a sign of sear, span,
His skin surface smooth without a burn,
Owning a whole estate like an emperor.

Everyone stares at him with utmost envy,
Young ladies want him at privy.
He murmurs a single word all remain meme
wordless
Thinking that he is proud like other rich but
careless.

His entry entices all but angers others,
Those who wildly cry in echo like echoed waters,
Not taking time to know the steps he took to
victory,
His sleepless nights and slow steps very scary.

His humble like huntsman beginning,
Years of his strange struggles so counterstaining.
His dark days of dauntless effort
Now relaxed, rich and an introvert
Enjoying after the enslavement like a servant.

I have held it within me.
    (James Safo)

In my hands, I have held it strongly
I am not withstanding weight prolonged
Carried my burdens bearing parried
Wishing that I had dared to dream huge.

It is precious, precarious and persuasive
I had yearned for it and I have it invasive
Its presence like precious a ring filled my mind
It has made me a man enough so difficult to find.

Many have referred me as refined as victory is
mine,
It's not a coincidence coined in time and me my
space.
What a jolly and joyous be envied by others.
Though intangible, yet I hold it
Am the victor holding the true success bolt.

99.

A wish for you.
(James Safo)

Never lose your strength,
For in doing so you will lose your breath,
That will deter your determination for self-growth,
You must remain forever focused and have faith.

Never ever, lose your hope,
For in doing so to failure your hoop,
Even if it takes your life-time loop,
Have courage to carry on your scoop.

You will be able achieve your dream,
If you dare to strive hard like a swam,
You will need a right start!
And a wonderful team to keep you alert.

100.

A smell of victory
(James Safo)

It very nicely near you than you feel,
It is coming easy for you have worked hard like a
squirrel,
It is meant for the determined,
Who remain on the course aligned.

For you have the required skill,
And the required strong will,
Undoubtedly its yours without fail,
Soon you will be full like a backfill.

Nothing will stop you from achieving,
You will succeed for you are striving,
Success comes easy for those who are trying,
Just remain strong and focused!.

101.

It is a share of ups and downs.

(James Safo)

It does not come in a silver platter,

It is a product of dreams almost shuttered,

At some point in time.

It has a share of ups and downs,

At some time loved ones disowns,

You for the feeling that you are a perennial loser.

It comes amidst struggles and strive,

In a world where everyone becomes,

overwhelmed by life,

And makes you want to be like everyone else.

Real victory means being content,

Knowing ones worth and value of every coin

spent,

So, take time and repent,

Start afresh and victory you will leap.

102.

Guts of victory.

(James Safo)

Deep within you lies a seed,

A seed so silent waiting for time of need,

When you are tired and about to quit,

That one gut of victory, have it.

You know that you can reach far,

If only you look at the star,

A tireless nature and a life of set goal,

Not sitting back and taking no role.

It is a gift for those who tire,

Who are not discouraged and retire,

So, let you goals be your determination,

For the time you feel to quit you are near the

destination.

104.

Destined for victory

(James Safo)

It's now clear that all ways of heaven are open,

All roads ready and cross the gleaming sky,

All heavens are ready, but you remain rear on the

way,

All determined to ensure your everlasting

success.

You think you are thick and doomed,

That you alone is the cursed,

Terror and triumphs seem are not to wait,

But the be sure the divinity has divided for portion

so don't hate.

You are silent and feel all knowing,

The reason God is sending trials following,

Every attempt to shine.

Dear friend you are not perfect from the ultimate

height of living,

Lightly turn through the muds and stumps loosely

hung,

Don't dare toss your ball and keep your own flag

flying,

The determined lord is down at your path and will keep you walking.

Chapter 4

Acknowledgement

This book is devoted to our creator who I serve as his slave.

I cannot compare myself to Jesus Christ or God's prophets up to prophet Muhamad who was believed to be the last prophet, and God revealed his Holy words the Quran.

But I can say that, the journey God has taken me through is equivalent to prophets Job and Joseph as reported in the Bible and Quran. The evidence will be in my autobiography.

I also accept the philosophy books on Buddhism, Hinduism, Sikhism and any book which highlights God's Ten Commandments in full to be practiced by their followers as a way of life. God accepted and gave human beings the choice of how, when and where they wish to worship, praise and Glorify Him. We must all forgive and love each other irrespective of faith, creed and gender so that we can be strong and united, in order to give us a chance to be selected to go to heaven on the judgement day.

On judgement day, it will take less than "15" fifteen minutes for all humans in the universe, dead and alive from when the first human Adam was created and the decision cannot be appealed.(I am being generous here), considering judgement will be delivered to everyone at the same time. I predicted in 2014 that only about 1% of people may go to heaven, which might even include people who practice the ten commandments but do not go to church or any worshiping place. There are too many false messengers and hypocrite who do not practice what Almighty God want.

Who is God

I regard "God/ Allah" as the Greatest architect, Geometrician and the Greatest overseer of the universe, omnipotent, just, holy, independent spirit, One, personal. God can hear, see, speak to, feel, smell, and control the actions of humans animals and plants at the same time.

He is Almighty, everlasting and Sovereign God.
He is the only one who can penetrate into the secret recesses of the heart of humans, because He is the head king, eternal, and immortal, invincible the only wise God, be the kingdom, the power and the glory for ever and ever.

Author Qualification

Author Qualifications

1. BA (Hons), Law: include Criminal, Tort, damages, Contract, Property, Equity and Trust, European law, Public, Constitutional, Judicial Review, Agency.

2. (LLM)Master of Law; on legal research, and business, CSR Corporate social responsibility and human Right law" Institutional development and management, International Law.

3. Advance Dip. Business Law, Level 4: include Employment, Agency, Damages, Tort, Contract, employment tribunal etc.

4. Dip. Criminology

5. BA (Hons)op. Account: Financial Accountant and Management Accountant

6. Cert. Acct; Professional Certificate in Financial and Management Accounting

7. Dip. Book-keeping, Level 3

8. Nursing: RMN (Psychiatry trained nurse)

9. General Trained Nurse

10. Cert. in Education (Lecturer)

11. Business Certificate in Advanced Management

12. Cert. Business Enterprise

13. Advanced Food Hygiene

14. Intermediate Health and Safety

15. Dip. Safety Management

16. International Entrepreneur for over 25 years

17. Computers'. Cisco Level 2 Technician, (build, repair, networking)

18. Dip. Clait Plus (in all software)

19. New Clait Dip. Level 2

20. Microsoft Specialist

21. ECDL Level 2

22. Script writing: Dip. TV, radio, stage and film

23. Non-fiction writing: Dip. Autobiography, Biography and Family History

24. Cert. in Counselling

25. Author/Self-Publisher: Over 30 books published (2020)

26. Plumbing: Level 3 City and Guild

27. Theology: Cert. Bible studies; researched Theology for my PhD (most faiths)

28. Psychology and Social Science (university level certificate)

29. Photographer: Portrait, Glamour and Figure Photographer (PGFP).Dip.

30. Dip. Hypnotherapy

31. National Vocation Qualification (NVQ); Internal Verifier, (V1)

32. Trainer and Assessor A1 (NVQ)

33. RMA Registered Management award

List of my published Books in 2019/20

In June 2019, I published the following books plus other books translated into Arabic, Spanish, French and Chinese, plus different formats such as eBooks,

Faith Books - in English Language

1. Love All Faiths

2. Faith Unity

3. Messengers

4. Islam v. Christianity

5. Allah Loves Islam

6. God Loves Christianity

7. God Enlighten Buddhism

8. Parama Nandra Loves Hindus

9. In Search of Wisdom in Freemasonry

10. Jesus Christ is Coming Soon

11. Psychology of Religion, Politics & Marriage

Non-Faith Books- in English Languages

1. The One - Over 130 Poems "DCF"

2. Mood Disorder

3. Sweet and Sour women (plus over 500 love letters from women)

4. The Law (Over 1,160 Questions and Answers)

5. set up and manage a business

6. How to set up a care home and care agency

7. How to manage a care Home and care agency

8. Care Home; Staff training

9) Criminology

10) over 150 Love Poems

11) over 100 poems on Faith and Victory

12) over 100 poems on racism, discrimination and suffering

13) Psychology of religion, politics and marriage

14) Law and Religion

The following are Translated completed and published books in June 2019.

The following translated in Spanish

1) Dios ama el Cristianismo (God loves Christianity)

2) V. Islamites Cristianismo (Islam   v Christianity)

3)) De la Sabiduria En la Masoneri

(In search of Wisdom in freemasonry)

4) Ame todas Las creencias (love all faiths)

5) Mensageros De Dios (God's Messengers)

6)) <u>Allah ama elIslam (allah loves Islam)</u>

The following translated in French

1) Messagers de Dieu (god messengers)

2) Islamisme. v. Christianisme (Islam v Christianity)

3) A la recherche de la sagesse dans la franc-maçonnerie (In search of wisdom in freemasonry)

4) Aime Toutes les Fois (Love All faiths)

<u>5)</u> Dieu Aime Le Christianisme (God loves Christianity)

6) Allah aime l'Islam (Allah loves islam)

Over 100 Poems on Faith and Victory   by James Safo

The following translated in Chines

上帝爱伊斯兰教 (Allah loves Islam)

伊斯蘭教訴基督教(Islam v Christianity)

The following translated in Arabic

الاسلام يحب الله. (Allah loves Islam)

الأديان جميع حب Love All Faiths